THE YORKSHIRE MISFIT 2

The Dales Will Never Be The Same Again!

C K Lobb

City girl, turned country bumpkin Jess, is no stranger to life's ups and downs. Now in her mid thirties, and not the slightest bit concerned about settling down, she decides to go it alone in the Yorkshire Dales, working as a self employed rural farm secretary. Her character can perhaps best be described as James Herriot meets Bridget Jones.

Some may call her difficult, some may call her feisty, others may see her as a bit of a stubborn, non- conformist but Jess is ok with being all of those things as she is no stranger to having to walk her own path without apology. Now at an age where she is less likely to give folk the benefit of the doubt, you are about to take a peek through the amusing daily lens that Jess cares to call her life, set in the rugged Yorkshire Dales

Unfortunately, the Yorkshire Dales is not quite ready for her no nonsense approach to life and ruffling a few feathers is the least of her concerns. This is a sequel of short stories about her daily life experiences that will have you giggling away in this Have A Laugh A Day Series - Book Two.

In book two we see Jess and her hilarious struggle on blind dates. In one chapter we even watch her break into her own home and in another she eagerly attempts to solve a murder mystery in the local town hall. Meanwhile, her encounters with Knuckle Scraping Bob will hopefully have you in stitches as he now appears to be a regular visitor in her life. Add to this her admittance of not strictly being from Yorkshire as she tries to fake it and her rescuing a farmer from a failed night fishing expedition. You will not fail to find humour somewhere amongst this little lot.

If you enjoy humour around everyday life experiences then The Yorkshire Misfit is the book for you! One short story a day guaranteed to give you a laugh throughout your week!

The Yorkshire Misfit Book 2 is dedicated to Daisy above, in her amazing canine life jacket.

'Up here in Yorkshire we don't sip, we slurp. We don't do drizzles; we do dollops. We don't do slices, we do slabs. We don't scatter; we pile. We also don't appreciate garnishes or have much respect for foliage or dressings or indeed anything that's green unless it's the great green Yorkshire soil that we firmly stand upon. Unless of course you're a Yorkshire guzzler; in which case standing firmly is particularly tricky.'

CONTENTS

COPYRIGHT

Editor/Author: C K Lobb
Proofreader: Kelda Yeo
Interior Design: C K Lobb

Imprint: Independently published
Have A Laugh A Day Series – Book Two

CHAPTER ONE – THE WINE DATE

'The room is now spinning just a little and I'm wondering if he can make it stop because it's not funny!'

◆ ◆ ◆

So there we are at the very posh restaurant and I've now drunk about half, of a half, of a pint of bitter and I'm strangely feeling decidedly tipsy. Suddenly it hits me. I'm taking some new tablets from the doctor and I don't think I'm supposed to be drinking whilst using them. There is a harpist playing in the corner of the restaurant, seated next to a large piano so you can tell how posh this place is. However she is merely adding to my dreamlike state. I'd better slow down but at least my blind date hasn't noticed as yet.

"So why don't you tell me about yourself?" he says, resting his chin on his knuckles, elbows fixed onto the table. I figure that this is the worst way to begin a blind date known to man. Why I hear you cry? Because he has already assumed a superior position with that very question. Now I feel like I'm on a job interview with someone who hasn't been bothered to prepare questions and so they want you (who is not being paid for your time and efforts) to tell them (who are being paid for their time and efforts) what they already know in the form of your CV which is sat right in front of them. Nooooooo thank you! You know what; I'm turning this on its head, quick style.

"I tell you what, why don't you tell me about yourself?" Now the power is now no longer his. It's now up for grabs. Halt! No, I stand corrected. The power now is still his as he is grinning and relishing in the fact that he is now able to twitter on about himself for the next hour. I immediately sense that I'm going to be sneaking home early tonight via some nearby fire exit. It won't be the first time. I'm well into double digits with this type of activity. You see already I have a problem and this is why. I should not date until they get to know me first, which I know defeats the whole purpose of a blind date. The thing is, if they got to know me first, they would know not to bother going on a date with me and we could all save ourselves a lot of time and money. But anyway here he is, here I am, and it's now time for the waste of time to actually commence.

The waiter comes over to the table,
"Your wine sir." He proceeds to pour a tiny amount of wine into a glass for my date to sample. To anyone who knows me; you may as well at this point pull out a red flag to a bull.
"Er, hello, I think I'd like to try some if you don't mind?"
"So you know about wine then do you?" asks Joe. At least, I think he's called Joe. I hope it's not short for Josephine. Well you can't be too careful these days can you.
"Huh! Do I know about wine? ....Do I know about wine? Why wouldn't I know about wine?" I actually know nothing about wine, except that I know it's made from grapes and you can have red or white. That's it! That's as far as my wine knowledge goes. But I'm not admitting that to this lot let me tell you.

The waiter pours out a bit of wine into both glasses and my date starts to spin his wine around in the glass, before delicately sniffing the contents thereof. He sounds like a piglet snorting for truffles, if only he looked as cute.

I grasp the stem of my glass in between my fingers, with my palm faced upwards and also start to spin. The spinning motion is making me feel quite dizzy as I'm clearly now under the influence and I prefer to knock up some speed to get it over with but I'm so fast some of it escapes from the glass.
"Oops a daises!" I giggle. I then take a sniff but I sniff much too quickly resulting in me snorting, not like a piglet, but like an almighty hog.

"Ooooo now then, there's a definite smoky smell to this one," I say excitedly. Josephine looks delighted, "Ah yes that will be the oak barrels," he declared knowingly.
"Now that smell; it's reminding me of something.............. Gosh what is it?"
"Oh it's just great when wine does that. It's the bouquet you see." He takes a delicate sniff. "Ah yes, the romance of Italy. The coffee filled cafes of Paris. The............. "
"Oh I know what it is!"
"Yes?" We were both getting excited now.
"Well, it was in the heat of summer......."
"Ok."
"Back in the seventies I think....."
"Yes?"
"There was this amazing sunrise. I remember all the sky being full of red and orange, with hardly any breeze at all."
"Yes..........yes," he said leaning in. He is now on the edge of his seat.
"Well that very same day................t'local gypsies came and tarmacced the whole of our council estate. There was smoke everywhere." I look wistfully into the distance and sighed blissfully.
"You can't put a price on memories like that!"
My date just stared ahead, speechless. No words. Meanwhile the waiter was grinning widely from ear to ear,
"Now then where was I?" I continue with my expert grape ana-

lysis at the table.
The couple at the next table are now listening to everything I'm saying but it's ok because as my therapist says; I need to start caring less about what other people think so I'm now fully operating under doctor's orders. There are currently no flies on me and the wine is certainly adding to the carefree attitude that I'm only too happy to embrace.

I hold the glass up proudly to the sky, my arm extended fully. I've no idea what I'm doing but I'm suddenly feeling extremely confident even though I think I'm struggling a tad with my shaking limbs due to the drug and alcohol combination.

"Now then," I announce, looking proudly up towards the glass. Well, I am a Yorkshire lass now that I've crossed the border from Lancashire and that seems to be the most popular phrase on the Yorkshire streets. I don't know what it means and I used to respond with "Now then what?" to which the reply is often "Nothing................ just now then!" I don't get Yorkshire folk. If you said that to someone in Lancashire they'd be expecting a conversation or at least a question mark added to the end of that phrase. But no, this is Yorkshire, where the use of words are scarce, and pockets with holes, even scarcer!

"Mmm...........fruity little number is this one!" I declare adamantly. Well I've got to be convincing, I'm taking no prisoners here. I take a very unladylike swig which is real easy for me as I don't tend to walk that path too well anyway. I think the tablets are having a slight effect on my motor skills now though as I'm struggling to get my lips to the edge of the glass. I begin to chew the wine across my palate and then proceed to hold it on my tongue a bit like my dog does when he has tasted some interesting urine outside on the street. You know when they repeatedly smack their lips together and they look like they're grinning. The look is quite fetching on my dog but I'm sure it's doing me no favours at this particular moment in time. I think I might need a straw to be on the safe side. Although I've got an issue with straws as

last Christmas I went to a pub with my friends and the bartender asked me if I'd like a straw with my coke?
"No thank you, I'm a grown woman, not twelve," I said smiling sarcastically.
"Sorry," he embarrassingly mumbled "but we've been told to ask all the ladies if they want straws with their drinks." We both roll our eyes in the air and snigger at each other. Confident that we are all capable of being better human beings, I turn to find my 47 year old friend sitting at a table, drinking with a pink straw and who has now proceeded to put her hair into pigtails! What the............?

However, I have just about finished my wine chewing before giving my expert analysis. I look and sigh. Meanwhile Josephine and the waiter along with the couple seated at the table next to us, eagerly await the verdict.
"Now then, unfortunately, I cannot taste even a single grape!"
I take another swig and chew. There is nothing but silence surrounding me now. I can't even hear the harpist anymore. It's just me, the wine and the sound of my gums smacking together. I place my glass firmly back onto the table. I look up sombrely, as if about to deliver some amazing profound knowledge on all things grape like. I eyed Joe and the waiter decisively.
"Nay, I don't like it!"
My date now has his head in his hands.
"But that's the finest wine we have in the house," grins the waiter.
"Yes but I happen to have extremely superior taste buds, particularly in the area of soft and dangly fruits," I respond seriously, burping at the end of my sentence and smiling sweetly to the waiter. You can now clearly see why I don't get out much and I think after tonight it's safe to say I'll be venturing out even less.
"Well would you like me to get you a glass of something else?" asks the waiter.
"Oh no, don't be doing that. Just add some tap water to it, it'll be fine."
"You can't put tap water in wine," retorts a stunned Joe.
"Well just stick some ice cubes in there then. Oh and before you

go, I don't mean to complain but why is this chicken pink?"
"Oh that's the way the chef does it here," chuckles the waiter.
"Why? Is he trying to save on the leccie?
"Oh my word," mutters Joe, shaking his head. I continue,
"Also, I can't make out a single tune from that woman in the corner with that big guitar thing. Is she playing any actual tunes tonight or what?"

The waiter rushes off.
"Are you ok?" asks Joe.
"Yep! .... This is fun! Aren't you having fun?" I'm now leaning back in my chair,
"Ey, I wonder how far back I can go on this chair?" I say toying with the idea.
Josephine is now sweating, twitching and looking a tad stressed.
"You seem a bit drunk," he says, looking very serious.
"I'll have you know............. I've been drunk...........never.............. once in my whole life, ever............. and I don't intend now to start! " I don't know how I managed to say that sentence without slurring my words but I did it! The room is now spinning just a little and I'm wondering if he can make it stop because it's not funny!
I then go to rest my elbows on the table and unfortunately my right elbow hits the end of the fork handle at my table setting, hurling it into the air and landing on the floor near the table behind. I turn around to the couple residing there.
"Oops a daisies. I couldn't just retrieve my fork could I? It's just there by your shoe!" The man slowly leans to his feet and passes it to me without breathing a word.
"Ever so kind. Ey, d'you know if they do chips here at all?" I ask innocently as I brush the fork against my top to clean it. They look horrified and don't even answer. I turn to my date;
"How rude are they?"
"Keep your voice down," he whispers.
"What?"
"You need to keep your voice lower," he leans in.
"You're gonna have to speak up, I can't hear you!" I shout.

"I said you need to lower your voice," he repeats.
"I can't, this is as low as I can speak," I say in the deepest voice I can muster.
He proceeds to take a deep breath and looks at his watch.
"Look, I think we best be off."
"Well I must admit, you are looking a bit blurry to me. Maybe you need to get yourself off home..............Well go on then, I'll see you around sometime."
He looks at me open mouthed.
"I'm not just gonna leave you here!"
"Oh ok, well I tell you what then; you stay and I'll go."
He shakes his head in disbelief, grinning and frowning.
"What's so funny?" I ask innocently.
"You! You're funny!"
"Well, I'll take that as a compliment if you don't mind," I grinned.
"You know, in a strange way, I actually enjoyed tonight," he mused softly.
"Eh?"
"Can I see you again?" he asks.
"Eh?" I look behind me to make sure he isn't actually talking to someone else. Nope, no one there!
"Like a second date?" he continues.
His words have the immediate effect of a triple espresso. Suddenly I feel completely sober and I know what I need to do. Looks like I'm about to notch up another double digit folks. Now then, the nearest fire exit please!

CHAPTER TWO - THE CAT BURGLAR

'The thing is, once you turn thirty, gravity is no longer a friend.'

◆ ◆ ◆

So I arrive home, late, from one of the farms where I work. One of the young farmers there was complaining that his girlfriend of twelve months; doesn't seem to realise that condoms have a use by date. For some reason he repeatedly insists on telling me about his romantic life. It's like this farmer the other day who was telling me about a young lad in the village who's got a young lass pregnant, who was, as he delicately put it, running his ferret without a muzzle! Why men keep talking to me this way, I have absolutely no idea! I think it's because they think I'm on their side which of course I am but only in theory. What I mean by this is, you want to side with them but you know it's within your best interests not to. I guess it's the equivalent to those men whom when asked, do they believe in equality for women; they answer,
"Yes of course, absolutely............well you know.......... within reason."

Anyway, I arrived home with my dog, absolutely starving and ready to get into my house only to find that I couldn't. As we approached the front door, my dog just froze right there and then on the spot. There was a cat sat there on my door mat! Nothing strange about that you may cry. The thing is, I don't actually own a cat. Not to mention the fact that my dog dislikes them intensely. I spend the next ten minutes trying to entice this cat away from the front door but it's having none of it, spitting and hissing. Blinkin eck! How the hell am I supposed to get into my own house? We're both starving! Of course if we weren't hungry and had plenty of time, this simply wouldn't be happening now would it.

I went around to the front of my flat, hands on hips, sighed and looked up towards the heavens. I don't know why I looked up, perhaps just asking God for some inspiration and you know what, I got it! My top living room window is slightly ajar, on its catch. Now then, if I could just get in through that window I could open the front door from the inside and entice the cat away. Yes, as I recall I have some tuna in the fridge which no cat could refuse. See now this sounds like an excellent plan. I'm one hundred percent certain that this will work. I do realise that all my plans tend to sound excellent in theory but more often than not, when in practice, it's a whole different ball game. But what choice do I have? Besides what could possibly go wrong on this one? I'm fit, agile, small, slim and as a kid I was the one of the best gymnasts in school. Besides I really don't fancy a cat bite at this precise moment in time.

I clamber onto the bonnet of my car which is parked in the driveway, below the window. This allows for some extra height to reach the upper window frame. I then take a deep breath, bend my knees, followed by swinging both arms swiftly up towards the sky before takeoff. I lunge my whole body towards the window frame and catch the inside of the frame with my fingers. I'm fairly pleased with the take off, all's well there but now I appear to be just dangling like a lifeless rag doll. Oh! Oh! I didn't think this through. What now? My arms after a few seconds feel like they are going to come out of their sockets and I realise that I rapidly need to produce some form of emergency dismount as I don't appear to actually possess the upper body strength that I thought I had, to hoist myself any further up. I have no choice but to let myself go backwards onto the bonnet. By nothing short of a miracle I dismount quite safely back onto the car bonnet. I look down to my dog, his eyebrows raised curiously. If he had a watch, he'd be looking at it right now and asking me how long is this going to take. He doesn't look impressed,

"Don't worry boy, that's just a warm up is that. I'm just getting the old limbs in gear that's all." I determinedly prepare myself to repeat the initial launching process, trying to put to the back of my mind the rather large dent I have now made in the bonnet of my car. How I'm going to explain that to the local garage I've no idea. I look up at the window determined.

Wow this is quite exciting, this is how burglars must feel. The adrenaline and the rush of it all. I mean, fair do's, I happen to be breaking into my own house and I know where everything is which I agree takes the edge of it slightly but still it's fun, as I'm now imagining myself as catnip for burglars.

I take another deep breath and on the count of three I cautiously launch myself at the window once more, catching the inside of the window frame with my fingers. I slowly ease my way through the window and would you believe it, the plan seems to be actually working. I now have one arm and one leg inside the window frame and I'm simply holding on for dear life whilst trying to wrench myself further through. Gosh I didn't realise I was still so nimble. You see this is when being a skinny runt really has its advantages. At school, when dealing with bullies I found that my nip and run theory worked a treat, by charging at them from afar, knocking them to the ground followed by some pretty sharp nipping action on the skin.

In fact, my cousin also carried the talent of a fantastic nip reflex and she was famously crowned The Nipper in close circles. I believe it's a genetic fallback as our Great Grandad used to rear ferrets. And I think his dad did too! Clearly the nip reflex has always been well regarded throughout our family history and has been passed down throughout the generations and eventually executed on a human scale. So I'm guessing it's genetically inbred. You can't make this stuff up you know!

Gosh I'm halfway in. I can't believe how easy this has been. Wow, I'm so agile. I'm nimble! I'm quick! I'm like shit off a shovel! I'm like a rat up a drain........Oh! Oh! I think I'm stuck! Holy cow! How the hell do I get out of this one? I look towards my dog now laid down by the car, dozing off and would you believe it, seated right next to him was that damn cat, licking its paws and yawning. Without sounding like Victor Meldrew; I don't believe it!

Suddenly, from nowhere, appears a small boy, about eight years old, looking up at me as I hang majestically halfway through my living room window. I'm now red faced, puffing and panting and can feel the sweat dripping down my back.
"Whatcha doing?" he grins mischievously.
"Never you mind what I'm doing. Haven't you got some doors to play knock and run on?"
"Nay, been doing that all morning. Bored now," he grins back.
"Look just go away will you. Go on, go away. Surely you've got some other poor sod to annoy."
"Nope, just you," he responds decisively.
The truth is I could actually do with a hand and he is clearly bored.
"You couldn't just grab my foot could you and hoist me up a bit?" I quiz.
Well now he looks positively ecstatic.
"Are you breaking in?" he asks, eyes shining in complete wonderment.

"Yes but it's my own............"
"I'll get my mates to help............"
"No, no, that's not nec............"
Too late. He was off screaming down the street.
"Lads! Lads! Give us a hand will you. Hurry up! Give us a hand!"
Before I know it there were a group of four lads pushing me up with their hands. I'm attempting to direct them.
"Ok, steady, steady. I SAID STEADY!................ Right that's it lads....................yep, keep going, keep going. Easy now..............easy......Ok, that'll do. No more pushing. (My jumper is now being ripped by the edge of the frame!)...........I SAID, NO MORE PUSHING!"

I'm now feeling the constraints of the window frame around my very own frame and I'm starting to get slightly concerned. I'm currently in a state of limbo. My brain knows where my body needs to go but my body is having none of it. I'm also aware that even if I can wriggle free, I'm going to struggle to make the last haul through the window as I'm lacking upper body strength which is a total lie by the way, as my upper body strength is fine and I know it's the weight of my backside that's really causing the problem and dragging me down. The thing is, once you turn thirty, gravity is no longer a friend. It's like a cruel thief in the night. One minute you're the fairest in the land and the next, even the mirror doesn't want to look at you.

The lads are now on their phones, calling their mates and taking pictures of me stuck halfway through the window. I was sweating and past caring. There is also now a small crowd beginning to form.
"She's locked herself out," I hear someone shout from the crowd. If only they knew I had a key. There was now even an ice cream van supplying refreshments, whilst groups of kids are taking photos and the elderly folk are handing out mints. An old lady looks up at me.
"Would you like an ice cream dear............you know, till the fire en-

gines get here?"
"Er, I'm a bit busy right now.......eh, hang on, did you just say fire engines?" I asked urgently. No sooner had I said it, I heard them. The dreaded fire engine siren. Now I know there is many a woman out there who would like nothing more than to be rescued by a team of brave fire fighters but I'm definitely not one of them. The sound of the sirens was the only motivation I needed. One almighty last push and I'm home free. I land in a cluttered heap on the floor. It wasn't pretty and it looks like I'm going to have to purchase a new TV however on this occasion I was pleased that my backside was able to provide ample extra cushioning. As I clamber to my feet, looking dishevelled and sweating with a torn sweater, I can hear the crowd outside. I wrench myself up to the window, feeling slightly unsteady, panting and red faced but I'm greeted with waving and cheering from the crowd. Ah, only in Yorkshire. I give a huge smile and a double thumbs up for victory. They cheer louder. Wow look at that crowd. They really like me. Told you! Catnip! I wonder if this will get into the papers? I'm nothing short of a local hero. You see us Yorkshire folk look out for one another. We care about each other. We're there in times of need. We always help each other and..........Crap! Has someone called the police on me?

Minutes later I was being interviewed by PC Twelve Year Old.
"So what made you want to break into your own house?" said the police officer looking very concerned at my dishevelled appearance. I shrug my shoulders. I've almost lost the will to live now and I can't even look him in the eye.
"I don't know.........just felt like it that's all!"
"So you do have a key then?" he queried.
"Yep!" I pronounce proudly, holding it in front of my face.
"So let me just get this right. You had a key and you still chose to enter your property by breaking in through your own window. Is that correct?"
"Cor.........rect!" I announce loudly, folding my arms defiantly. I am now the twelve year old. I turn away at this point due to complete

embarrassment. I realise that he must think I'm insane. At this moment in time, I would agree. He stares hard at me.
"Do you have any mental health difficulties that I need to be aware of?" he asked gently.
"Of course not! As if! Well, I mean yeah, I may have a bit of OCD, ADHD, ADD and I struggle with PMT and now no doubt PTSD after this lot but who doesn't have all that in this day and age mmmmm?"

I was hoping to distract him with all the acronyms but I realise that I'm now looking completely crazy to the outside observer. He kneels down to face me and looks at me gently and with deep concern.
"Look around you. Your sweater is ripped. Your TV is all smashed up. You've broke into your own home. It's not looking good dear. Can I ask; are you on any type of medication?"
I look at him innocently.
"No," I said quietly.
He leans in, "well dear, may I suggest that you perhaps seriously consider it."
I look back at him blankly. There are no words. Fair cop!

CHAPTER THREE – CALAMITY JESS

'He'd steal the steam off your porridge would that one.'

◆ ◆ ◆

So there we were; me and John (farmer), with his walking stick, walking in single file, back to the farmhouse, down this narrow track. He was showing me a field to his right, and as I looked to the field, prompted by him pointing to it, he decided at that very moment to bend over and pick up a stick. What is this obsession that farmers have with sticks anyway? As I wasn't looking ahead at the moment he decided to bend over, I found myself quite speedily catapulting head first, over his back. I landed very quickly, at his feet, in a clattered heap on the floor. I looked up at him angrily,

"Why the hell would you ask me to look at something over there and then decide to bend over? For God's sake, I nearly broke my bloody neck!"

"You nearly broke my back an all. By 'eck lass, how much do you weigh?"

After a few more, shall we say, un-carefully chosen words, we eventually arrive back at the farmhouse. John hobbles out back for 10 minutes worth of sheepdog training which is really 10 minutes of 'owner training' by Jip, his mischievous Border Collie whilst I go inside to see his wife, Barbara.

"All right Barbara," I shouted as I enter the farmhouse kitchen.

"Now then Jess, could you get some pitted dates for this Farmers Ball as our John and his dodgy bowels will be attending and they tend to get him working," she asks.

"Too much detail is that," I grin back.

I turn to the farmhouse kitchen window to watch Jip the sheepdog, train John; how she can get away with as much as possible. Suddenly, he's tripped over by her and falls flat on his backside. Huh, hopefully she stopped to pick up a stick!

I turn to Barbara;

"Barbara! Barbara! Come quick! John's just fallen down. I think you need to............"

She takes a quick peek, "Oh he's fine, don't worry about it."

"No but Barbara, he's not getting up......I think he's struggling......"

"Oh he always does that. Now then do you want cake with your cup of tea?"

"No, I'm on a diet but John.........."

"Oh, he'll be all right. He did the same thing yesterday. He was out there for a good twenty minutes.........I watched the whole thing right from here................." I stared at her blankly. She continued, "...............and it was snowing! Oh by the way, I know you've just moved so I was wondering whether you needed any pans for your new house? We've gone out and bought new ones," she continued completely unconcerned.

"Er, yes, I won't say no to a set of pans. Thanks very much; that's ever so nice of you," I answer, still keeping my eye on John struggling outside.

"Oh don't mention it. They're ok, it's just that the non stick coating is coming off and so there were bits of black stuff getting into our food and you never know what harm that can cause do you. Anyway, there you go, I've put them in a bag for you!"

Eh? I stare at her curiously, as she faces the window, watching Jip

playfully tugging John's trouser leg whilst he still attempts to get up off the floor. Barbara and I have never quite got along and I can't quite put my finger on what it is.
"You really love your John don't you?" I ask inquisitively.
"What do you mean by love exactly?" she squinted sharply.
"Well you know; you couldn't live without him." I continue.
"I live without him everyday dear. He's never in the house. Spends more time out with them there animals than me."
Ah avoidance. I recognise that bullet as I often try to dodge it myself but mine is more like the bullet of denial. I believe that denial is a very close friend of avoidance and almost sits on its tail. I press on.
"How long you been married then?"
"Oh I'm not very good with dates," she declares dismissively. She clearly doesn't want this conversation and I know I'm annoying her with all my questions. It's not that I purposely go out of my way to annoy folk but when they clearly don't seem to like me for no apparent reason; it's sometimes a lovely by product. So; I press on.
"Well you must have been in love when you got married though?"
"Oh Jess," she grimaces, "Sweet, sweet, naive, gullible.......................silly.................silly Jess. Folk didn't get married in those days for love."
"They didn't?" I ask half innocently.
"Of course not. It's well, it's what folk did then. It was expected." she sighs.
"Yes but you must both sleep in the same bedroom though?" Yes I realise this is pushing it a bit but I get the distinct feeling that I'm being patronised.
"Course we do, we're not Victorian's dear." She leans in close. "And I kid you not; sometimes I can even feel his leg over on my side of the bed..................which is no easy feat when you consider that we've had a 3 drawer chest separating our single beds for the last 2 years. Anyway, tea?"

Suddenly John appears from outside.

"Ey Barb, this hip must be getting better, only 10 minutes out there today."
"Was it really snowing yesterday out there then John?" I asked genuinely concerned.
"Aye lass but it was warm snow." Ah, only in Yorkshire are we apparently blessed with warm snow.
"Now then I've got a treat for you two. Don't go anywhere." He limps out of the kitchen and heads upstairs.
"Oh Jess," he shouts, "Bob is outside doing some labouring. Keep your eye on him will you. He'd steal the steam off your porridge would that one."
Moments later, John appears from upstairs, in his musty old suit for the Farmers Ball - think Freddie Star in the eighties!
"Can you believe this suit is from the seventies?"
"Yep," shoots Barbara, eyeing him up and down.
"I've still got it!....... I've still got it!" He does a funny jig.
"Bout time you got rid of it then," she sniffs.
"Are you going t'Farmer's Ball then Jess?" asks John.
"Nope! The very title of the event rears up imagery that's not best left to the imagination," I shudder.
"Eh, you never know, you might find the man of your dreams," grinned John.
"Eh, what makes you think I dream about men?" I wink at Barbara and laugh. Get this! She winks back at me and doesn't laugh. Blinkin eck! Is this some sort of code? Am I missing something here? I immediately feel myself starting to sweat. Is she? Could she be? No......delete that. It's just my imagination! She's happily married to John. Correction! She is married to John. Heck!
"The only available man round here is Mr Archer," adds Barbara. I try and regain myself.
"He's an asthmatic eighty two year old." I laugh.
"Yeah but last I heard, he's thinking about settling down," insists John.
Mmmmm I think I'd rather date Barbara!

Two cups of tea later, I was busy working alone, on my laptop at the kitchen table before the infamous Bob enters, no doubt to annoy me as usual. Needless to say Bob and I do not get on. I don't know what it is. Perhaps it's the way he always appears from nowhere. Perhaps it's the way he stands with his hands low down on his hips. Perhaps it's his broadened stance, or maybe his cocky attitude, or maybe the way he walks with an overly wide gate, or maybe it's the way he holds his arms out to the sides as if he is carrying a large carpet roll under each armpit. Ok, so maybe I do know what it is! I don't know if he has a horse saddled up outside but he's wearing one of those tool belts; that holds tools that hang down that no one ever really uses and we're only short of a saloon door and tasselled chap type trousers and were now in John Wayne verses Calamity Jane territory which is so unfair on John Wayne as he really doesn't stand a chance. I mean let's face it; that's not even a fair fight! The fact that he is chewing on a piece of straw (Farmer's gum) merely adds to the effect. The only equivalent weapon I have is the pen that I'm holding in my hand so I too, proceed to chew on the end of it. We can't have Calamity Jane being outdone by John Wayne otherwise we'll have to rewrite cinematic history and that's not about to happen on my watch!

We eye each other whilst chewing. I can almost hear the soundtrack to 'The Good, The Bad and The Ugly' in the background. We take turns squinting our eyes at each other and if we could go back to back now in a standoff, we would. I don't like the fact that I'm seated and he is standing which clearly gives him the edge but I'm too busy squinting and trying to chew my pen and I'm not a woman for whom multi tasking is easy. In fact I'd go so far as to say multi tasking is a dead end job but promoted as a compliment to get us ladies to do more. Thankfully this cowgirl ain't having any of it! He then proceeds to grab one of the chairs from the kitchen table and places one foot onto the seat, with bended knee, continuing to smirk and chewing his gum. "Now then!" he announces. Well today, I'm wearing my Craghopper trousers, with Lycra extra stretch and elasticised waist as I plan to go out for a big meal later and I like to be prepared. Two words; GAME ON!

The air is still as I take a despondent sigh whilst slowly easing myself up from my chair. I also place my foot onto the seat of my chair and lean in towards him. "Now then what?" I ask. Of course, I realise we both look utterly ridiculous but this is now about pride and power; and not to mention, a perfect opportunity to see how much give my new trousers have for some good old Yorkshire grub later on. Suddenly John walks in and we both panic, knowing he would have a fit as we are both on the clock.
"Yes Bob," I announce; "these are extremely strong pine chairs." I proceed to tap the legs of the chair against the sturdy farmhouse kitchen floor whilst Bob just stands nodding in agreement, both his feet now fixed firmly to the floor.
"Just need a pen. Well, its grand to see you two getting on for a change," grins John, grabbing a pen off the worktop and exiting again. I turn to Bob angrily;
"Listen up, wise guy. Spit it out! What is it you're after?"
"I want this in that there oven," he reveals, passing me a ready-made meal. No please. No thank you. No nothing. He rudely nudges it onto the kitchen table.
"Er, I'm not sure," I say looking around for Barbara. "I don't know how to use the oven."
He leaned in, "Just use your instincts lass," he antagonised. Why, what do you know, this rootin' tootin', no bit scoundrel, thinks he's a funny guy. I'm seriously thinking this cowboy needs to head on back to the windy city (in his case Leeds) coz this town ain't big enough for the both of us! He continues to stand before me enjoying the moment, half grinning and yet also, half sweating in anticipation of my response. There are two words floating around in my head right now. The second word is off and the first word sounds like duck.

The air is still as I take a huge despondent sigh whilst a slow grimace appears on my face. Everything is now happening in slow motion. A tumbleweed slowly makes its way through the kitchen as a cool breeze wafts through. I'm sure I can make out a church gong in the distance which only adds to the impending darkness

of this highly volatile situation or maybe that's just in my head but still..............I like it! I glide quietly towards the kitchen window, as though appearing to be on roller blades, as Bob watches with baited breath as to my next move. Even the birds outside have stopped singing and there is a deep, dark calm encapsulating the whole farmhouse. You could literally hear a porcupine pin drop! Birds flutter frantically back to their nests as Mother Nature knows that there is something afoot. I too know that there is something about to happen when I start to use words like 'afoot'! I slowly turn around to meet Bob's gaze. Someone is about to get hustled and it ain't gonna be me. Facing him head on and taking a slow deep breath, I smile and say,
"You know what?"
"Whaaaaaaat?" he mocks.
"I am sooooo attracted to you right now!" He takes a moment to absorb the un-absorbable.
"Eh, what's that now?" He almost looks behind him which, let's face it, is completely understandable.
"I'm so attracted to you right now," I repeat.
"Get out, you're winding me up. You're..............."
"Oh, I know how the local women folk refer to you as a pot bellied piglet but not this one." I proceed to gently prod his stomach with my pen. "To me, that's something to keep me warm in winter is that. And those man breasts of yours. They're nothing short of tender headrests and your receding hairline; well, (I'm struggling now!).........what can I say.................what can I say........... So then; how about it? Me and thee, farmer's ball, this weekend?"
I wink at him and he is definitely sweating now. Oh I love it when a plan comes together. The hustler has now become the hustled! This is what it's all about. You know life is really worth living for with moments like this. Ah, I can almost taste the sweetness of victory, the smell of success; the...........................
"Aye, all right then lassie."
"Eh?"
"You know, I always knew you had a thing for me. All this tension between us. You know what this is don't you?"

"No," I say defiantly.
He leans in.
"Lust!"
So I guess it looks like my secret love is no secret anymore then eh? Now let's get some perspective here. He's either; A. Rustling up a double hustle. B. He really is as stupid as he looks and doesn't understand the situation. C. My money is on B. or D. Other – only the sweet Lord will ever truly know!
"The things is, I usually only date pretty women," he continues quite confidently, "but I'm prepared to make an exception for you." Why the no good, rotten scoundrel.
"Ah, so you only date pretty women do you?"
"Yep!" he says adamantly.
"So, the saying must be true then. Opposites really do attract!"
He looks at me blankly. Never has the phrase 'over one's head' rang more true than in this moment. He absolutely has no idea what I'm talking about. A worm that lives in the pocket of another worm; that lives in the pocket of that worm, would certainly have more brain capacity than this bizarre specimen stood before me right now.
"Count me in, should be a good un' and wear a nice dress. Don't forget that oven now will ya love. Oh and you might just want to take a quick look in the mirror."
He waltzes off, gait wider than ever and whistling. Holy cow, what have I done now? I've just arranged a date with this............ this............worm of darkness. Oh clever, clever, me! Suddenly, the prospect of going to the Farmer's Ball with an asthmatic 82 year old is now looking highly attractive let me tell you. I sigh and look in the mirror just hanging over the Aga.............what the?............................I only have blue ink all over my chin from all that pen chewing.

John hobbles into the kitchen.
"Well, are you still the fairest in the land? he grins. I tell you what, being out there on the floor today has really knackered my hip?"
Ey up; now's my chance to find out a bit more about Barbara.

"Ey, John, do you have life insurance?"
"Aye lass you can't take any chances these days."
"No indeed! Ever thought about cancelling it?"I probe.
"No why?" he said puzzled.
"Nothing, no reason."
"Anyway, you ought to come to this ball lass," he continued. "It would be a great way for the locals to get to know you and let's face it; you're not getting any younger yourself."
"Sod off you. I'm only thirty five."
"Yes but think of it this way. If you snuff it at 70 you're half way through your life now. In fact; you could quite easily be middle aged as we speak."
The kitchen goes quiet as I seriously contemplate the possible prospect and the associated impending doom that befits some-one of middle aged status, not to mention the date with dark-ness that I single handily arranged all by myself. Heck, that was possibly a senior moment which I probably could have handled much better just five short years ago. All I can envisage right now are false teeth, liver spots and hip replacements. The future does not look rosy! I note the cream cakes on the kitchen side that I had refused earlier. I turn to John;
"Oh screw it, I'm middle aged, bring on the fats!"

To be continued ....

CHAPTER FOUR – MURDER MOST FOUL

'You're as skinny as a bread stick from t'side on you are.'

◆ ◆ ◆

So I arrive at the town hall wearing the most stupid looking ballroom dress you could imagine. It looks like a tent made out of purple felt. I don't want to be here. I don't want to be wearing this.......this..........velvet tent thing and I definitely don't want to have to meet the infamous, 'knuckle scraping' Bob!

I'm referring to the evolutionary scale of which he is firmly placed at the lower end of the continuum if you get my drift and therefore standing upright is still a tad taxing for him. I'm just about to head upstairs when I see a group of ladies in the lift waving me over.

"Hop in Jess," shouts Doris from her wheelchair.

"No I'd rather not. I'm not a fan of lifts actually."

"Oh, you'll be fine. Just squeeze in next to me dear," she insists.

I sigh and take a deep breath. Perhaps just this one time I'll make an exception. After all it is a social gathering and I'm supposed to be acting sociable but I've never been one for conforming as most of my friends will tell you. Oh and when I say friends. That's a lie! I mean friend. I don't have that many friends which is completely by choice you understand. Ok, that's another lie. It's not completely by choice. You see the very definition of being a misfit is that you don't fit into society too well so you're kind of on the outside looking in. But I'd rather think it's society at fault and not me, then that way I'm not completely one hundred percent strange; perhaps just seventy five percent strange. Ok, eighty percent but that's as high as I'm prepared to go publicly. Fair do's though, privately it's more likely to be in the region of ninety five percent strange but that's between me and thee.

Anyway I don't know why I find being sociable such hard work. I find it so tiring talking to folk and trying to feign interest. And yet I talk to myself all day long, no problem! The hours quite happily fly by. Thankfully, we don't need many words here in Yorkshire, as we like to conserve our energies for our harsh winters. We enjoy eating too much to spend time chatting and we're also strong believers in winter plumage and that's why we have sooooooooo much time for fats. Without this staple diet of fats; the Yorkshire population would surely die out. It's perfectly simple. In Yorkshire; we need, nay demand, our fats! It's not that we don't appreciate the nicer things in life though. I mean we can stick out our little fingers out with the best of 'em and we have been known to enjoy the odd glass of Pimm's now and then but deep down, we're not sippers; we're slurpers. A number of us, who prefer to remain anonymous and hide in the dark shadows, are even guzzlers. It's the same with food. We don't do drizzles; we do dollops. We don't do slices, we do slabs. We don't scatter; we pile. We also don't appreciate garnishes or have much respect for foliage or dressings or indeed anything that's green unless it's the great green Yorkshire soil that we firmly stand upon. Unless of course you are a Yorkshire guzzler; in which case standing firmly is particularly tricky.

Anyway, as the lift doors slide ever so tightly shut; I notice not a single gap around them. Air tight is the immediate phrase that

springs to mind. Well isn't this just dandy? The lift swiftly swings into action. I'm now ignoring the general conversation within the confined space of the lift and adhering to my therapist's orders, concentrating on deep breathing and counting to ten. However at number five; the lift jolts to a complete standstill.
"What's happened?" I gasp holding onto Shirley.
"I think the lift is stuck," she answers, pressing the lift's buttons at random.
"Stuck! You're having me on?"
"Oh no, not again," cried Doris.
"What d'you mean................not again?" I shout.
"Oh, it always does this. It's a tad temperamental," reassures Doris.
"And you tell me this now knowing that I have a fear of lifts?"
"Well it's OK. You've got us lot for company," confirms Marion, pressing the emergency button to call for help.
I inhale a deep, purpose filled breath, "I don't need company. I need oxygen!"
My breathing is slightly laboured as I peer around the lift anxiously; eyes widened and my mouth is seriously starting to go dry.
"Ah, is she panicking?"grins Shirley.
"Yes; yes; she is!" I shout. "Please do join me!"
I place my hand onto my neck. Ok I still have a pulse so I think that must be a good sign.
"Oh you'll be fine. You can't run from your fears all your life dear," preaches Marion.
"Course you can. You just put one foot in front of the other and move pretty sharpish. Done it all my life. Never done me any harm." I turn to Doris; "I don't suppose you've got a bag I could breathe into have you?"
"Well," said Doris, completely ignoring me and reaching for her knitting from her handbag, "they don't tend to rush do these rescue folk."
"I'm not standing here waiting for the rescue crew," I cry.
"Well sit down and wait for them dear, unless you want to get

yourself through that hatch up there for the safety release button," she suggests, pointing to the roof of the lift.
I glare back at her. Blimey, I'd like to see my therapist try and talk her way out of this pickle. No air, no deep breathing. No deep breathing, no relaxation. No relaxation, enter hyperventilation; whom I'm certain will very soon decide to pull up a chair. Heck!

"Eh, did you hear about poor John Metcalfe? Fell downstairs last week you know," gossips Shirley.
"What, you mean Barbara's husband?" asks Marion.
Suddenly my ears prick up.
"Yeah; all she kept saying was that's why they call 'em slippers but guess what? I've known John Metcalfe all his life. He doesn't wear slippers. He's always worn trainers. Never owned a pair of slippers in his life," muses Marion.
The whole lift goes quiet as we all contemplate the possibility of some kind of foul play.
"I tell you what though; that Barbara; she makes a good trifle for t'Farmer's Ball every year. I'll give her that!" chips in Marion.
You know I don't think I can take much more of this.
"Right, that it! One of us is going to have to get up there to that hatch thing and reach for that safety button and my money's on you Shirley. You're clearly the lightest here and we could all just lift you up quite easily."
"I'm not going up there. I'm eighty two!" she yells, horrified.
"Well you're only as young as you feel that's what I say."
"Yeah well, I feel ninety two!"
"And I'm in a wheelchair," sniffs Doris, "so don't look at me either."
"Marion? What about you? You could squeeze through that hatch up there no problem. You're as skinny as a bread stick from t'side on you are."
She grabs me by the arm;
"Jess; you're the youngest here. You know it's down to you dear."
I stare at her in despair. For God's sake, since when did I become the captain of the over seventies squad? I didn't sign up for this you know.

What can only be described as a Trump baby strop moment, I immediately turn to the panel of lift buttons and I aggressively press every single button, some of them simultaneously just for the sheer hell of it. Would you believe it, miraculously the lift actually shifts into gear and starts to move. Now that we're thankfully on the move I'm starting to feel a little ashamed of my irrational behaviour. The others cheer and clap.
"Are you ok Jess now that we're on the move?" asks Shirley looking quite concerned.
"Course I'm ok. Couldn't be better. No fear here!" I lie. Gosh I'm really sweating now. I hope we're out of here soon as I'm not sure how much longer I can keep up this pretence of bravery. I may as well be stood here with a staffie or pit bull wearing a T-shirt and a baseball cap with the words 'No Fear' in large print. The lift doors open and I casually stand there. "Well then you lot; off you go! There's no fear here!"
I lean casually against the lift as if I'm quite happy. They take for absolute ever to get out with every passing second more painstaking than the last.
"Aren't you coming out then?" asks Doris.
"Yeah I'm just, you know, securing the lift. Just taking my time. No worries! No fear here!" I announce, stretching and yawning to promote the idea of being carefree and nonchalant. As I place my hand back down to rest on the wall of the lift, I inadvertently press the lift buttons with the palm of my hand and would you believe it; the doors swing tightly shut and I'm off again. God damn it!

Moments later, I'm almost crawling on all fours out of the lift, feeling very woozy and a little breathless but thankfully free at last. Suddenly I hear a scream coming from the ballroom. Holy cow, what fresh hell is this now? Hopefully it's just one of the old dears getting worked up because we've ran out of cake or something. I enter the ballroom to find John Metcalfe keeled over by the trifle, at the buffet table, with a crowd around him. He's always fooling around is John and this is so typical of his behaviour. "Oh he's having you all on," I say, walking casually over to his lifeless body, "You all know what he's like. Now then John lad, this is no time for napping," I joke nudging him, "There'll be plenty of time for that later when t'chairman does his annual speech." He is not at all responsive and slumps even further down into his seat. I instinctively reach to his neck to feel for a pulse. Oh! Oh! There doesn't appear to be one. I look back to the crowd;

"I can't feel a pulse!" I say breathlessly; my voice shaking; "What happened?"

"Shall I call the police Jess?" asks Shirley.

I nodded, my eyes wide at the shock of the situation. All eyes are on me. I'm now Inspector Clueless which is a role I know I can definitely excel in. I begin to pace up and down because that's what all the great sleuths did in a crisis. Apparently it gets the old grey matter working.

"Sooo now then......." I've no idea what I'm doing or saying but we're in Yorkshire and the phrase 'now then' always seems a good place to start. So confidently, head held high, shoulders back, I begin to pace.

"So what do we know?" I ask the small gathering.

"We know that John is dead," a voice shouted from the crowd.

"Yes besides that; what do we know?"

"We know he had bowel problems," shouts another.

"Holy cow; besides that?"

"We know that the trifle didn't agree with him," shouts Doris, her eyebrows raised at me knowingly.

The trifle? Of course! Barbara? Where is Barbara? I'm now putting two and two together and unfortunately getting four.

"Is Barbara about?...........anybody?" I desperately shout out.

"She went home she wasn't feeling very well," shouts a voice from the crowd.

"Maybe she ate some of the trifle," sneered Marion.

"Oh I very much doubt that," I say confidently.

"Why do you say that then?" asks Doris.

"Let's just say I have a hunch that's all."

"And have you had it seen to?" leans in Shirley.

A few folk from the crowd look as if they are about to leave.
"Hey, where d'you think you lot are going? No one leaves until we find out what's gone on here. For all we know this could be a mmm......." I stop short as I realise the seriousness of what I'm about to say. Doris looks up at me from her wheelchair, wide eyed and almost visibly shaking.
"What? You don't mean?" asks Doris.
I nod. My mind is dizzy with racing thoughts.
"I mean murder, Doris Dinglethwaite. Murder most foul!" I say loudly. The crowd gasp aloud, with lots of 'ooing' and 'aahing.'
The room falls deadly quiet. We all eye each other suspiciously. The silence in the air is broken by a door creaking open on the other side of the hall. We all turn to spot old Mrs Hall coming from the toilet.
"Ah! Ah! Mrs Hall, and where were you two minutes ago?" I probed suspiciously.
"I just nipped to the loo," she said innocently.
"And why did you decide to do that at the exact moment that this dastardly deed occurred?" I continued to quiz.
"Well I had a call of nature dear."
"Mmmm, a call of nature you say. I'll just make a note."
This is now beginning to resemble a scene straight out of Midsummer Murders.
"Is he dead?" stammers Mrs Hall, "Poor John, spent so much time on the old throne and now reduced to this. At least now his bowels can rest in peace," she says with a sniffle.
I spot an elderly lady in the corner of my eye, just about to indulge in the trifle.
"Don't eat that," I yell, "there could be something wrong with it."
She stood with the spoon; mid flight, en route to her lips.
"Well I was right looking forward to that an all," she said disappointedly.

I continue to pace the floor, my mind awash with ideas and

thoughts about Barbara Metcalfe.
"Now then," I proclaim; "I'm going to map out where we all were when this grizzly murder occurred." I don't know why I'm talking this way but there is a part of my brain that thinks it actually sounds good. However it's the same part of my brain that still thinks I look good in ripped jeans.
Suddenly the ball room hall doors burst open with a bang. It's Barbara! She comes running in with a male companion by her side. A very handsome male companion at that.
"Is he ok?" she shouts running towards us all.
"Well well well; what took you so long to get here Barbara?" I shout.
"I had a flat tyre on the way," she blurts out breathlessly.
"Ah! Ah! A flat tyre you say? I'll just make a note."
"Why do you keep repeating everything?" shouts out a voice randomly from the crowd.
"Why do I keep repeating everything? I'll tell you why I keep repeating everything because this is a murder scene and you, Barbara Metcalfe; you have some explaining to do."
I eyed the good looking bloke up and down. Well today I'm an inspector and if that means having to inspect handsome men then so be it. It's also absolutely imperative that a thorough inspection is done. After all, I'm just doing my job you understand.
"And who is this may I ask?"
"I'm a doctor!" he answers confidently.
"A doctor you say? Mmm interesting. I'll just make a note."

Suddenly, from out of nowhere, John raises his head from the table. A scream along with gasps of "It's a miracle!" fly first hand from the crowd. I catch my breath as I stare at him, completely dumbfounded.
"Blinkin eck; so you're not dead then?" I gasp.
"No, I think I must have choked on something," he spluttered, holding his throat.
"I think you'll find this is what you choked on," interrupts the doc holding a small stone between his fingers.

"Right so that means the trifle's ok then does it?" says the elderly lady still standing by the trifle; spoon at the ready.
"Oh you're such a good doctor," purrs Marion, fondly stroking his arm.
"Forget it Marion," spits Barbara, "he's married."
"Oh I do love a challenge!" she smirks.
"That's a date stone," claims Barbara, taking it from the doctor's hands. "We always buy pitted dates though because of this very reason and we.................." She stops mid sentence and slowly turns to me.
Ah! Ah! I mean, Oh! Oh! I think I may need to leave this so called 'murder' scene. Inspector Clueless has just remembered that she purchased the stoned dates a few days ago, as they were much cheaper than the pitted ones. Well we are in Yorkshire and I'm trying to blend in.
My inspector instincts tell me that I now need to proceed with some immediacy towards the nearest exit and never, ever leave the house again unless in disguise. Which brings me right back to why I don't socialise in the first place.

However, it seems that Satan has not finished with me yet! There is a tap on my shoulder. I swiftly swing around and come face to face with knuckle scraping Bob. The evil has landed.
You know I'm seriously going to have to have words with the big guy upstairs because when we last spoke I specifically asked for just one problem at a time and he clearly didn't listen. I'm now having to think fast on my feet.
"Now then lass; I believe I was promised a date?" grinned banana boy.
"Ah yes, so you were," I point over to the dish of dates. "There you go, take as many as you like lad."
At that, I turn about heel and immediately flea from the town hall passing the ambulance and police parked up outside. I thought it best that I make myself scarce as I don't want to meet the same copper who caught me breaking into my own home a few weeks back as he suggested I should start taking prescribed medication

ASAP. I think this time he may want to possible begin committing me into some specialised unit after this lot. I sneak off into the cool night air. I really need to go and have a lie down. I think I can safely say with much certainly that I'll not he getting an invite to the Farmers Ball next year. I think once word gets out about tonight I'll never have to decline an invite to a social gathering again as the chances are, in true misfit style; I'll not get asked. The legacy lives on!

CHAPTER FIVE - YORKSHIRE VERSES LANCASHIRE

'I don't even like the word mingle. It sounds like a disease.'

◆ ◆ ◆

It doesn't matter how many times I roll my eyes, check my watch, check my phone, stretch or yawn, this elderly farmer continues to talk. He is stood on the nice, firm grassy verge leaning on a farm gate, whilst I am on the very un-firm, muddy compacted soil side. The weather is the hot topic of conversation and so naturally, and ask *any* farmer about this one, everything else pales into insignificance.

This particular farmer, Jack, lost his wife last year and must be feeling quite lonely up here on this very remote farm and I really don't want to appear rude so I let him carry on talking about the weather, then land prices and then the price of sheep, oh and then back to the weather again. It was only when I noticed that I appeared to be shrinking in stature, due to the surrounding mud, that I became slightly alarmed. I attempt to move my boots and realised that there was a distinct possibility that I may be ever so slightly stuck. The temperature also declines very quickly on these hilltop farms which isn't helping the situation much either.

I notice his large shovel hands as he rests them on the top of the gate; his knuckles reddened and raw, protruding from his sausage like fingers, which no doubt could tell many a tale of the physical toil they have endured over the years. Completely exposed and attacked by the elements until suddenly they seem to have no feeling in them at all. It's getting colder but having spent most of his life working outdoors, he really doesn't seem to notice.

They were an unusual couple; him and his wife. I remember she would often repeat everything he said.
"Nights are drawing in lass," he'd say.
"Aye nights are drawing in," she'd repeat.
"You'll be having trouble getting back down that lane," he'd say.
"Aye trouble back down that lane you will," she'd repeat.
There was never a question of whether they got on or not; they just somehow, well got on with it regardless. I'm not saying that's right. I'm not saying that's wrong. I'm just saying it was what it was!
He is still talking and I've realised that I'm now beginning to sound like his deceased wife.
"At least land prices have stayed the same lass," he muttered.
"Ah yes, they've stayed the same all right," I responded reassuringly.
"But I've still got my eye on those new inheritance tax laws," he squinted peevishly.
"Oh yes, those inheritance laws definitely needed keeping an eye on," I insisted.
Gosh is it possible she was just humouring him all these years? She wouldn't be the first woman on that score though would she, let's face it!

Suddenly he decides it's time to move.

"Now then lass, I can't be standing here all day talking to thee. I know how you ladies can talk once you get going!" My mouth opens to reprimand him but I'm simply not quick enough. I tell you what for an old bloke with a cane he can certainly shift. I look down towards the farmyard about 300 metres away as the old farmer makes his way back down the hill towards the yard. There is however, another figure on his way up. Oh no, that's not knuckle scraping Bob carrying his carcass over in my direction is it? Bloody hell, it is! It's him! I can tell by the way he rocks from side to side and his stupid wide gait. Why oh why, does it have to be this very moment when I'm stuck that he decides to appear on the scene? You couldn't script my life you really couldn't. Who knows, maybe someone will write a book about it one day. No but that's just crazy talk. Like that's ever gonna happen!

Bob is getting nearer and there is nothing that motivates me more to shift my backside than seeing someone whom I really don't want to talk to. And as a Yorkshire Misfit let me tell you, that happens much more than I care to mention because I've noticed something rather strange going on. The more you keep your distance from folk, the more interesting you actually become. It's true! It's one of those things that no one ever tells you because no one wants to admit that they're slightly anti-social or that they're not good at mingling. I hate mingling. I don't even like the word 'mingle.' It sounds like a disease. It suggests closeness and folk invading your space. Well let me be the first to say it. I'm currently single and I'm not wanting to mingle!

However I have to say that living in Yorkshire does help us misfits though as we're not quite shall we say, 'at one with the words.' A nod, a finger held up at the steering wheel whilst driving (unless you're the farmer Jim, from Lancashire, who lost half his forefinger in a farming incident, in which case he holds up half a finger) or the odd cap raised and that'll do for us. As for humouring folk, well that's different to being humorous isn't it? I can be humorous but I can't humour anybody. I just can't do it. It goes against every natural whim I possess. Take me and knuckle scraping Bob for instance. It would truly harm me mentally to have to humour him and hold it in rather than doing what I enjoy the most; delivering any humour at full throttle. He is still making headway towards me by the way but I think his knuckles scraping the floor might be slowing him down a bit so that's truly a blessing as it buys me a bit more time to think through my strategy. I try to move my wellies again but they are definitely stuck rigid in the mud.

The prospect of having to take my wellies off is not appealing as I note the swamp like conditions around my feet. I try to pivot just my upper body as I swivel round and I can't believe how flexible I actually am. Hey that's not bad. I used to do yoga you know and I don't think you ever quite lose a basic foundation of flexibility. Now then, time to do the other side. With absolute confidence of being the yoga master that I once was, I swing my upper body confidently in the other direction as I'm hoping this will create some movement further down. I immediately hear a sudden crack. Oh! Oh! That doesn't sound too good.

However, pain takes a second seat as the angel of darkness himself has now appeared in front of me.
"Now then lass, what happened to that date you promised me?" he sniggered.
"I've no idea what you're talking about. You must have been dreaming about me again," I say stiffly.
"You're stuck aren't you?"
"Of course I'm not stuck. I'm simply enjoying the view!"
"What; the pig yard, the sheep dip and the scrap heap?" he yells amusingly, pointing down to the farm.
"If you must know I'm a great believer in recycling and a huge fan of pigs. Highly intelligent are pigs you know. In fact they're more intelligent than many people I know. People who are currently within stone throwing distance I might add."
"Hey, are you calling my dad a pig?" he shoots back, pointing down to the elderly farmer in the farm yard.

"Your dad?"
"Aye, it's my dad's farm is this," he said proudly.

Funny, I never pictured him actually having a mum and dad. I thought maybe he'd been created in a test tube in some far away, prehistoric, caveman type land where dinosaurs run free and men still grunt and carry clubs. It's not a pleasant image.
"Sure you've not just been eyeing me up whilst I've been working away down in that yard," he winks. You know it never ceases to amaze me how cocky some men are. I mean I don't know where they get it from but I too possess the 'skills' to play that game. The thing is if you're confident enough you can tell yourself anything and believe it, that's for sure. The question is; how much confidence do you have to actually believe your own hype?

For instance, as kids, my dad used to tell us that we lived in the countryside. We had this tiny bedroom window where if you looked way off into the distance from our council estate, you could see the black and white dots of cows being taken in to be milked. Not only did he have me believe that this meant we lived in the countryside but I was about 10 years old before I realised that cows weren't thumb size!

I can see Bob eyeing me up and down so I immediately and purposely deliver the same look back. I slowly veer my eyes from his head to his feet and then back up again. Game on!
"Like I said, I'm passionate about pigs. The four legged variety not the two legged," I smile smugly back at him. Well I may be stuck in the mud and bloody freezing but the old hat rack is still working perfectly well let me tell you.
"You're gonna have to do better than that to offend me," he says with a huge grin.
"I haven't even started tying to offend you yet!" I snap back.
"I think me and you got started on the wrong foot," he mused.
"I don't think so. I think we've started on the right foot actually and long may it continue."
He stares at me for a few seconds which seems to last for an eter-

nity. I'm now getting annoyed, bearing in mind I am still stuck in the freezing cold mud.

"Are you trying to think of something to say right now and your brain isn't quite quick enough; or is that you simply prefer these long silences?" I enquire quite seriously.

"Looks to me like you're stuck and you're too stubborn to admit it," he argues. He suddenly, without warning, pounces to the floor and grabs at my boots.

"Hey, what d'you think you're doing?" I shout angrily.

"They're stuck! Stuck fast are them chuffers!" he yells gleefully.

I pretend I hadn't noticed.

"Oh gosh, well would you look at that. Huh, fancy that!"

"Right, hop on then. I've not got all day." he murmurs.

"Eh?"

"Hop on, I'll piggy back ya down to yard," he says, turning his back to assume the position.

"Do your pigs fly?" I ask innocently.

"Duh, no!"

"Well only when your pigs have the ability to fly will I be accepting a piggy back from you!" I snap back.

"Suit yourself lass. The night's drawing in and it's getting cold. I think those hungry foxes might be out and about later tonight an all."

"I happen to like foxes!"

"Fair enough then lass. I'll leave you to it," he smirks, walking away.

He's now getting to me and he knows it. Whilst I do like foxes I don't really want one gnawing at my limbs if you know what I mean. There is now a cloud of fog like mist with every word spoken so it's definitely getting colder.

"Right ok, you win. Piggy back it is but I don't want this round the village in the morning. You know, acting like you're some kind of hero."

"Hero eh? Didn't think of it like that," he grinned. "I'm wanting that date though lass."

"Fine! Let's just get on with it shall we?" I yell in frustration.

I slowly and methodically climb out of my wellies and clamber my up a few rungs of the gate and then ease myself onto his back. I can tell he is as happy as a pig in muck and I can almost feel him grinning. I just know this is gonna be round the village by tomorrow morning. We're half way down the hill heading towards the farm yard and he's now puffing and panting.
"By 'eck lass; how much do you weigh?"
"I weigh the perfect amount for my perfect frame and my perfect height thank you very much. You're not getting tired are you?" I grin.
"Don't know the meaning of the word," he pants.
What he doesn't realise is that I'm making myself heavier like you do when you're a kid and your parents are trying to pick you up off the floor but you're too busy having a baby strop and relaxing your whole body so that you're almost impossible to shift.

We eventually reach the yard and he drops me off at the farmhouse door with an almighty sigh, as I dismount.
"Right well, thanks for the lift," I say.
"No worries, thanks for causing my back to go into spasm," he groans.
"Not at all," I grin. "Always a pleasure."
There is a moments silence between us. It's almost embarrassing. He nods, turns about heel and walks off without saying a word.

I enter the farmhouse and head straight into the kitchen where his dad is.
"Right then Jack, are we all set for this meeting then?" I shout, rubbing my hands together and trying to get warm. The farmers meeting starts at 7.30pm and every single clock in the house says 7.15pm but I know it's really only 7pm as all the clocks are set 15 minutes fast as most farmers firmly hold the belief that they can actually beat time. Show me a farmer who doesn't think he can beat time by moving his clocks forward and I'll show you a farmer who doesn't like shutting gates.

Anyway, the meeting eventually begins and there are about 10 of us seated in a very comfortable environment. China cups, tea, cake and a very dignified collection of rural eccentricities I might add, seated in a horseshoe circle. But I must warn you, the evening is about to change as good old Bob, whom I think is secretly employed by Satan, decides to drop the biggest clanger that will change everything in Yorkshire for the rest of our days. I was just saying to the group, whilst sipping a very posh cup of tea in a real china cup; how proud I was to come from Yorkshire when suddenly I spot Bob lurking about in the background. I continue and then he rudely interrupts me.

"You're not from Yorkshire! Can't you all tell? She's not got you all fooled has she?" booms Bob, grinning vindictively from ear to ear. They all suddenly stop talking and stare at me as if some massive crime has been committed.

"That's just soooo ridiculous," I snap, glaring at him, "I'm Yorkshire born and bred." I finish off my sentence with raised eyebrows and I'm feeling pretty chuffed with myself for reacting so swiftly and with complete Yorkshire passion. I majestically dunk my biscuit firmly into my tea and then proceed to take a bite out of it, only to find that I'm now snapping air as there is no biscuit actually present. The biscuit has decided to take a dive into the China cup and has definitely not had swimming lessons. Well, there goes my credibility for starters. I glare at Bob and then look back to the motley crew. They look aghast.

"Is this true Jess?" asks the group secretary.

"I won't lie to you," I lie. "I'm from you know Yorkshire.......ish."

"She's from Lancashire! I've been doing some digging!" declares Bob proudly. "I think we ought to build a wall to keep those Lancashire folk out," he jeered. Well red flag and bull is now the only image I can see before me. I completely and utterly take the bait.

"Huh! A wall wouldn't keep us out," I scoff. "That'd just be an extra challenge! And us Lancashire folk love a challenge which is why we eat tripe and black pudding."

"So it's true then Jess?" asks Jack gently.

"It might be," I say weakly, feeling rather ashamed.

"Yeah! And she was seen in Lancashire at the weekend too; in one

of their tea rooms," continues Bob gleefully.
"And was it Yorkshire tea you were drinking?" squints the group secretary. The group almost hold their breath awaiting my answer.
"Yes of course! Oh, absolutely! (I had no idea) Without any shadow of any doubt!" I turned angrily to Bob. "Haven't you got some pigs to be mucking out?"
I'm now being scrutinised in every possible way. If they had a spare lie detector hanging around right now, they would most certainly have me strapped to it. Why I'm defending myself I've no idea but I'm now being made to feel like I've betrayed the whole of Yorkshire.
"So were you in Lancashire at the weekend then Jess?" quizzes the secretary again.
"I was but only for one night."
"You mean you spent the whole night there?" she continued.
"Yes but honestly, it meant nothing.............I was thinking of Yorkshire the whole time!"
"And long has this been going on?" asks the secretary.
"Oh I don't know...... a few months maybe."
"And when were you going to tell us about these secret rendezvous across the border?" shouts a voice at random.
"Oh well, you know .... er, never."
There were now gasps of shock from the group. Cups were being placed firmly back onto their saucers as a declaration of some kind of state of absolute emergency.
"Ever heard of the war of the roses Jess?" leaned in Bob, still grinning by the way.
"Nope!" I say adamantly. "I've never been one for horticulture thank you very much."
"See, this is the younger generation for you," hurls out a blurred face from the group. "They know nowt!" Again another insult thrown at me! Right, that's it. I've had enough of this. I'm going in!
"Hey, I know how to accept folk as they are. Well, excluding Bob over there. And I know how to treat people as I find them. I might not know much about the war of the daises but I don't judge folk

just because they come from somewhere else." They all start to argue amongst themselves. Bob looks ecstatically happy as I glare daggers at him. You know where he can stick his date with me now don't you?

"Now look, hang on a minute," shouts Jack, "Have you all forgot? My wife was from Lancashire and you all accepted her!" He turns to Bob. "And you should know better lad; what with your mother having come from Lancashire. She'd be turning in her grave if she could hear you all right now. I'm ashamed of you all, I really am!"

The room goes quiet and they all start to look a bit guilty. Jack puts his back to the crowd and delivers me a cheeky wink.

"Well, perhaps we were being a bit harsh. Sorry Jess!" says the group secretary.

"So Jess, there is just one question I have to ask you though," interrogates Jack, "which do you prefer; Yorkshire or Lancashire?" The group are on the edges of their seats. You could almost hear a pin drop as they all wait with baited breath for me to answer. This was the true test. The final hurdle.

"Well," I muse, "that's for me to know and you to find out isn't it!"

CHAPTER SIX - THE SHELL OF YOUTH

'Leonardo Leonardo out!
Tinky Winky in!'

◆ ◆ ◆

So here we are; me and the good looking farmer's wife, trying to make small talk in the farmhouse kitchen. I am appallingly bad at small talk and hate those social situations where you feel obligated to speak to fill in any silences. She is also not one for small talk so we both just sit there staring at each other, fully aware of the awkwardness as we await the return of her husband. Well, I figure there are 2 approaches here; either you babble your way through or remain true to yourself and keep one's gob shut. Unfortunately I'm one of life's babblers.

"So, word is, you're a bit of a looker!" I shoot over to her. She smiles at me knowingly. Great start but never fear, it's me, Jess and this is not an American ending. "You know when you were younger I mean." The smile immediately turns to a scowl. "Not that you're not a looker now. I mean, you're a very, very, attractive women. Well you know, for your age. Not that I'm saying you're old or anything." Her eyebrows are rising ever higher which is amazing when you consider the height of her eyebrows in the first place. Let's just say she constantly looks permanently surprised and leave it at that. I haphazardly continue, realising that I'm now on borrowed time. "I don't mean that you're old or anything. You're very young looking, you know in an attractive way. Not that I fancy you or anything like that. I mean I bat for the same side as you do. Not that there's anything wrong with batting for the other side, well you know, if you like that kind of thing. Each to their own and all that eh!" I've no idea what I'm saying and I'm now quickly entering gabble overdrive. Once the gabbling starts I'm usually spiralling downwards at a magnificent pace. I try to change the subject. "So what do you make of the whole gay thing then? I mean currently, I'm batting for neither side if you get my drift.............. Well, I think I've made myself clear."

Stan thankfully comes back into the kitchen just in the nick of time.
"Are we all right ladies?"
"Yes, Jess and I have had a lovely chat about her being gay," his wife states confidently.
"Eh?" I swing round to face her quickly.
"Well that doesn't surprise me I've had my doubts for some time now I have to say," he muses quite seriously.
"What d'you mean? What doubts? Why? Where? When? How?"
"Well, you just give off a certain vibe, you know."
"What kind of vibe?" I demand.
"Well," he ponders "a gay one!" chuckles Stan.
Anyway, I don't mind if folk think I'm gay. In fact it could work to my advantage if the scourges of the planet like knuckle scraping Bob found out. Life would be positively bliss.
"You know, I think it's time I started fishing again," ponders Stan. "I haven't fished for the last few years and I don't really have any hobbies."
"What about your shell collection?" I ask. Stan does have some quite beautiful and rare shells that he has collected over the years and he is really quite proud of them.

"I think he means something a bit more daring Jess. He turns sixty next month and he's trying to recapture his youth," quips Jane shaking her head.

"Ey, I think I still have my wading suit!" shouts Stan, like an excited five year old. Five minutes later he appears in what can only be described as some kind of green, rubber, telly tubby type, wading suit.

"Blinkin eck! Where's Tinky Winky?" I grin.

"Tinky who?" It's wasted on him.

The rubber suit squeaks every time his thighs move and from the back he looks like he is wearing a nappy with a baby romper suit over the top. The rubber suit also stinks of, well, rubber. It's oversized and he looks utterly ridiculous but get this; he thinks he looks the business.

"Mmmmm..........I think I might need to invest in some new fishing rods," he ponders.

"I think you need to invest in a full length mirror first," I shoot back.

"Well I think he looks manly," purrs Jane. "Look at him; he thinks he's that grizzly bear fella."

"You don't mean Bear Grylls do you?" I snort.

I'm now losing the will to live as he struts his 'manly' stuff up and down the farmhouse kitchen. How can any woman consider that manly I ask you? I think, and I've thought this for some time now, I was definitely at the back of the queue when female hormones were being dished out.

"You're only going down t'river," I scoff.

"Yeah but I'm going to go at night," he said proudly.

"Ooo; night fishing. You are brave Stan," oozes Jane.

"Brave? It's only a mile down t'road," I laugh.

"Eh, that river can be dangerous if it gets high you know," he said, his eyes gleaming excitedly. Now then I'm gonna need my infra red goggles, whistle, compass, map.............." He's off! World of his own! His wife leans in and whispers;

"Do you think he'll be ok Jess?"

"Course he'll be ok," I confirm quite confidently, "everyone's always ok in telly tubby land."

It was just the very next day I happened to be walking down the main street when I spotted a green mass of rubber, squeaking its way down the high street. In fact I heard his squeak before I spotted him. Fishing rods over one shoulder, fishing bag over the other and fishing nets strapped to his back, with a walk so cock sure of himself that it would put even knuckle scraping Bob's strut to absolute shame. Adults are stopping and staring. Kids are waving and shouting; "Look, it's Dipsy!" As I stand there grinning, watching the squeaky green mass disappear into the distance, I immediately sense a feeling of complete and utter darkness surrounding my whole being. My world suddenly turns dark. Even the birds have suddenly stop singing and are scattering to their nests. Wow! It's like the lull before the storm! I veer my head ever so cautiously to the right............and there lay the answer. The prince of darkness himself. Bob! Even mother nature doesn't like him and she's never wrong.
"Well tonight's the night," he enthused.
"For what?" I sigh despondently.
"Got a date!" I turn to him, completely speechless for a few seconds as his beady eyes squint peevishly back at me.
"What, you mean a real human being?"
"Aye."
"From this actual planet?"
"Aye."
"Of the female variety?"
"Aye. A real looker an all," he gloats.
"So she has a guide dog then does she?" He either ignores my comment as he doesn't get it or he is just that incredibly arrogant he chooses not to acknowledge it. My money's on both.
"She's a good looking lass I tell you that for nowt."
"Well she'd have to be. She can't possibly have much brain power, going on a date with the likes of you."
"Sounds like someone's jealous."
"Jealous? Me? Sounds like someone's using big words they don't

understand."
He turns to look at his reflection in the bakery shop window.
"Yep! I'm definitely the fairest in the land," he sighs.
"I'm surprised you even have a reflection."
"You never know," he winks, "Tonight just might be the night." He raises his eyebrows in a suggestive fashion.
"Ah that! Well, I'd apologise for your performance in advance if I were you," I grin back smugly. "Tell her from me, not to worry though. We all have to rough it a bit sometimes."
"Ey, what about it lass; me and thee one night?" he winks.
"Sorry but apparently I'm now gay. It happened just yesterday. I've no control over it. It's just the way it is. See ya!" I waltz off down the high street. Beat that monkey boy!

At last I get to the end of the day. It's around 9pm at night. All is calm and quiet. Wait for it though. The phone rings and to my annoyance it sounds like some kind of heavy breather. Anyway I thought I'd engage in a little role playing and do the same thing back. Well how else are they gonna learn? I'm considering asking the caller what he's wearing but no; that would be rude. Whoever it is suddenly hangs up. Job's a good 'un!

I remember my gran a few years ago saying that she really wanted a 'booty call' as she was struggling with her high arches and instep and needed some advice. I tried explaining to her what those calls were really about but she was a bit naive like that. I'm a bit like that though. It must be genetic. You know that book, 50 Shades of Grey? You know what I think of when I hear folk talking about that book? Dulux Paint! I seriously wonder if there really are 50 different actual shades of grey? I also think that the big fluffy cute dog would definitely know the answer to that question.

Anyway, I'm just basking in my excellent criminal diversion skills and then the phone rings again. Crap! Here we go again. Round two. I roll my eyes at my dog and see that he is just finishing off a juicy dog biscuit and notice that he is also panting. You know what happens next don't you? I do what any reasonable,

sane thinking, mature person would do. I simply hold the receiver to the dog's breath and grin. Geez, I should teach a course! After a few seconds I place my ear to the receiver which is now covered in dog saliva by the way, and I actually hear my name being spoken albeit somewhat muffled and then I realise, its farmer Bear Grylls!
"Jess is that you? You're breathing funny lass."
"Oh er, sorry, just having a bit of an asthma attack thing." I start coughing to make it sound a bit more convincing.
"What's up? D'you know what time it is?"
"No, I've lost my watch in the river."
"Are you ok?" I ask. Silence.
"Are you ok?" I repeat. I can hear splashes of water and the wind howling in the background.
"I lost my balance Jess. Fell in t'river.................that's how I lost my watch."
"So what happened to farmer Bear Grylls?"
"He sodded off when it got dark, that's what happened. You couldn't pick us up could you Jess?" My heart sank. I've only just this minute sat down.
"But is your wife not home?"
"You're joking. I'm not telling her. It'll be in the village magazine will this if she has 'owt to do with it. Come quick Jess. It's pitch black out here."
"Ah is someone scared of the dark?" I tease.
"Aye lass."
"Eh?"
"I'm scared of the dark Jess. Never used to be..............I think it might be.................well, you know."
"No," I sigh.
"Well you know," he repeats.
"Er, I'm still on no!"
"My age Jess! My bloody age! I'm as blind as a chuffin' bat without my glasses. Used to have excellent night vision and now it's all gone. I got dizzy in the water, got fixated on the current and fell over. Luckily my wading suit saved me but I lost my grip and landed in what I think are giant rhubarb leaves. I tell you what;

this suit's chaffing my chuffing thighs an all! Come pick us up Jess................but don't be telling anyone will you. I trust you Jess lass. I trust thee." Oh no, a compliment followed by a request of some sort. Don't you just hate that? You've got the most gorgeous hair and oh, by the way, can I borrow fifty quid? You get the idea.

When I pulled up in the car outside the woods, it was a cold, still moonlit night. I could see the puff of my breath in front of my face as I eased myself through the gate to follow the path that leads down to the river. I looked up at the moon as it gazed back down at me. Wow it's very dark but that amazing blanket of stars is truly a marvel to behold. I take a deep breath as I grab hold of the gate. God know what state I'm going to find him in. The moon's gaze reflected back at me, almost lighting the way. It's a pity Bob isn't here as I've forgot my torch in the hurry and my mobile battery is running low. I believe that Bob's rapidly balding but exceptionally shiny head would surely reflect the moon's rays and help light the way. You see in an absolute emergency he would certainly have his uses.

It was just me and the moon at this point as I walked along the darkened path with Stan on loud speaker attempting to guide the way. It's hopeless though. We're spending most of our time repeating the line, "Can you hear me now?" Then I have a thought.
"Stan, blow the whistle you've got. Blow the whistle!" I shout into my mobile. Gosh I feel like I'm in the film Titanic, except a telly tubby now plays the role of Leonardo DeCaprio. Story of my life is that. Leonardo out! Tinky Winky in! Geez, I hope I don't find him in the cold river desperately clinging to a raft of wood. You know where I find him? In the cold river desperately clinging to a raft of wood. He can barely blow the whistle. He looks a right proper sight.
"I can see you," I shout. It's ok, I can see you."
"Quick Jess, I'm freezing my nads off," he shouts. I stop in my tracks. Again any romance in the Titanic film has now gone right out of the window for me I have to say.

And there he was. A mere shadow of the green rubber mass he once was. His rubber suit is now torn, as he clings desperately to the embankment on the river. His suit of green mixes quite well with the giant rhubarb leaves, acting as excellent camouflage. I didn't know whether to laugh or cry. It takes about forty five minutes to get him out of the river and back to the car.

We both sit there, staring silently ahead. I'm cold, wet, covered in mud and not best happy. He turns to me solemnly.
"'Ere you go Jess, you may as well have this." He reaches into his pocket and hands me this small but very stunning shell from the river bank.
"What's that for?"
"It's for you lass. You were right. I'm too old for all this now. It's me and my shell collection from now on."
"Well then, you keep it...................you know, for your collection."
"No lass. It'll just be a reminder of my old age. You keep it Jess. It'll be a reminder for you that life is short and all that." We look at each other intensely as he hands me the delicate shell.
"You're not wanting to hug us or anything are you?"
He laughs, "No lass. Just get me home...........get me home." As I was driving him home, I realised that it was twenty years since I'd watched the film Titanic. Can you believe it? Twenty years. I truly do not know where that twenty years has gone. I look at the shell on the dashboard. You know, I'm going to keep that shell hopefully for the next twenty years if I can and maybe, as corny as it sounds, tell the story of how this tiny 'shell of youth' possibly changed two people's destinies.

CHAPTER SEVEN – THE WOLF IN SHEEP'S CLOTHING

"I'd remove it now if I was you or your highly inactive and questionable wedding tackle, gets it!"

◆ ◆ ◆

It was midday by the time I arrived in the farmyard of Sunnyhill Farm to visit the farmers, Ian and Mary. They aren't the easiest of folk to get on with but this is Yorkshire and we tend to live side by side with folk quite harmoniously. Well unless they're from next door in Lancashire of course, then for obvious reasons, that's quite a different affair. Don't get me wrong, we will still be courteous. We might be proud folk but we're not arrogant. It's not that we don't welcome folk into our green and fair county and it's not that we don't trust folk. We do. But there is something about Yorkshire that makes it almost vulnerable to the outside world and I think I know what that thing is. It's our quirkiness. In a world where everyone wants to be the same; we don't mind standing out from the crowd. We know that folk don't often understand our way of life or the language that we use and that's fine with us. We won't apologise for it but it's ok. Perhaps we would feel better if we could ask some quick questions before entry is allowed across our border. Questions such as; (answers in brackets)

1. Which county do you feel is superior - Yorkshire or Lancashire? (Yorkshire)
2. Define superior? (The best)
3. Explain the phrase; 'Now Then?' (Ey up)
4. Explain the phrase; 'Ey Up?' (Now then)
5. If you have one wellie that is waterproof and one wellie that isn't waterproof, what do you do? (Put a plastic carrier bag over your foot before putting your foot back in the wellie that isn't waterproof)
6. Why is the word t' of real importance in Yorkshire? (Keeps our sentences shorter. We're not one for 'the words')
7. How do Yorkshire folk prepare for the winter? (Eat plenty of fats in summer to accumulate winter plumage for winter and then maintain it through winter which basically means we stay tubby the whole year round - it's the Yorkshire way!)

Enough said?

Anyway, it was one of those grey, grim and cold, overcast days that we're all too familiar with here in Yorkshire. There I was walking through the farmyard, just about to pass the parked up sheep trailer, when I suddenly hear;

"Psst!........Psst!"

I turn around. No one there. I carry on walking gingerly over the uneven cobbles and there it is again.

"Psst!........Psst!"

It appears to be coming from the sheep trailer. I tiptoe back and cautiously peer inside, in between the metal, trailer slats; to find numerous sheep staring back at me combined with the odd bit of scuffling and bleating. And then to my astonishment I spot an actual pair of human eyes glaring back at me. My breath catches in

the back of my throat;
"Who's that? ....Ian?............... Ian?.........Is that you?"

We are now staring, steadfast and wide eyed, eye ball to eyeball.
"Aye lass," he whispers breathlessly, "my hips have gone again. Get me the hell out of here will you. I can't feel my bloody legs."
"What ya doing in there? Shall I call an ambulance? Are you ok?"
"Nay lass, don't be bothering folk. Just open them there trailer gates."
I rush round to the back of the trailer and open the trailer gates to discover him crouched on all fours, arse end facing the descending sheep ramp. He remains perfectly lifeless on all four pins. I shout,
"Gates are open......whenever you're ready." He doesn't move.
"I said whenever you're ......"
"I heard thee! I heard thee!" he yelled irritated. "Give us a minute will ya lass. My bloody legs don't seem to want to shift." He proceeds to do this weird, on the spot knee shuffle whilst remaining in an all fours position. The surrounding sheep are becoming a tad excitable with this new manoeuvre.
"Look, shall I call for an ambulance?"
"There's no need for all that. I'll move in a minute. Don't rush me!" he snaps.

It was a very long minute whilst I just stood there staring at his backside I have to say. He stays almost lifeless, entrenched in the same position. It wasn't pretty! This farmer has had hip problems for so long now that he's almost developing a hunch back from using the whole right side of his body to help him carry his knackered left hip. He brings a whole new meaning to the phrase; 'if it ain't broke, don't fix it!'
After another bout of shuffling he slowly eases his way out of the trailer, backwards on all fours, down the trailer ramp. The sheep are becoming even more excited as he begins to back up down the ramp. Some of them are clearly feeling a tad amorous as they try to mount him.

"Get 'owt of it.................get 'owt of it I tell ya! Get 'em off me will ya!" It was at this point that I desperately wanted to laugh. I tried to help but my giddiness made the attempt half hearted at best.
"I hope you're not finding this funny. I only went in to read a sheep tag for your bloody paperwork," he scowled.
"Of course not! It's not funny on any level at all," I respond, grinning from ear to ear. "Why can't you just go and get your hips sorted?"
"I've told thee. I'm not wasting NHS resources on something that isn't an emergency," he cried.
"Not an emergency? You've just spent God knows how long on your hands and knees in that trailer with your sheep for goodness sake!"
"Aye well, it came over raining. Wanted some shelter any rate."
"Are you scared or something?" I ask "Because the NHS are very good and..."
"Scared? Course I'm not scared!" he interrupted. "Why on earth would I be scared?"
Ok, so clearly the man is scared.

I shake my head in disbelief. It's quite pathetic really. The lengths he will go to so that he doesn't have to face his fears are staggering to me. And this is what makes him so annoying on so many levels. Well that and his driving of course. He's well known for it round these parts. Get stuck behind him and you know you're going to be late. The thing is he drives everywhere at the same snail like pace and has been crowned locally with the nickname Speedy. I'd hate to see him on the motorway and I can well imagine him starring in the film Speed, except it wouldn't be a bus it would be a clapped out old Land Rover with a Yorkshire farmer and his tweed cap at the wheel. I can imagine Keanu Reaves shouting,
"You've got to stay above twenty miles per hour or the bomb will go off!"
"Nay lad, if tha' goes over twenty, it'll start costing me. Diesel ain't cheap round here tha knows." He doesn't need cruise control in his vehicle. He has his own unique method which basically is

never getting out of second gear. Maybe he thinks bad things may happen if he goes over 20 mph. Keanu would not be impressed!

I know his wife also finds him annoying. You see, although Quasimodo has his physical disabilities to contend with, he is nothing short of a psychological wizard when it comes to argumentative confrontation. Like Quasimodo this farmer is prone to deafness but unlike Quasimodo; his affliction is of the selective deafness variety. Indeed having been married for forty five years he is a well rehearsed practitioner of selective deafness. His wife can be often heard shouting,
"Can you hear me? I said can you hear me? Are you listening to me? I may as well be talking to my bloody self" Alas no response. The psychological master of silence is at work.

Getting back to this hip problem, I actually watched him just a few days ago carrying a bucket of cow's milk from one end of the farm yard to the other to feed the calves, followed by his very willing and loyal sheepdog, Meg. He was swinging his whole body as he tried to compensate for his bad hip; simply highlighting the protruding hunch developing on his back as he lowers his body to gain some momentum to the swinging motion. He was almost dragging his left lower limb behind him, across the cobbled courtyard. It was beginning to look like a scene from The Hunchback of Notra Dame; what with the backdrop of the old farm buildings and its silo tower and the grim, misty Yorkshire weather circling the farm. But alas, there would be no bell ringing today as Quasimodo is too busy with his farming duties. The milk is going everywhere except staying in the bucket whilst the very obliging Meg is more than happy to engage in a spot of housekeeping by cleaning up the milk trail with her tongue. The look on his face when he eventually gets to the calves with hardly a drop of milk left in the bucket is priceless. Meanwhile Meg was sat devotedly by his side licking her lips ready for round two of the best game ever.

Anyway I help him back into the kitchen as he still struggles to

stand upright.
"How long are you going to carry on like this?" I asked.
"If I can walk, I can work!" he growls.
Well there you have it. He just needs a job now with the Department for Work and Pensions, and they can adopt his 'If You Can Walk, You Can Work' philosophy as their new assessment criteria for Universal Credit. Champion!
I shiver as I realise its getting darker and cooler up here on the farm.
"Will you be getting those lambs in tonight? It's gonna be a cold 'un," I ask Ian.
"Nay, they'll be fine," he grunts.
"But it's gonna be minus figures up here."
"I said they'll be fine," he glares.
I glare back. Remind me again why I don't particularly like this guy?
"Your paperwork is in a right state you know."
"Well that's what I'm paying thee for."
"Yes but you're meant to maintain it yourself otherwise it takes me much longer which means you'll get charged more." He completely ignores me.
"Right; let's get this paperwork sorted out for this sheep count next week then."
Suddenly, in the corner of my eye, I see something move, just by the Aga in one of the numerous wicker baskets. I rub my eyes and try to re-focus. There is it again. Gosh, I hope it's not rats. You all know how I feel about rats. I go even colder at the very thought.
"Ian! Quick! Look! There's something moving over there!" I gasp, pointing over to the collection of wicker baskets by the Aga, many of them covered.
"No there isn't. You're imagining things," he snorts defiantly.
"I'm telling you there is something moving in those baskets!"
"Oh there's nowt there. Come on now, into the office whilst we find this paperwork. I don't have all bloody day," he barks.

Funny how he can move quick when he wants his own way! But

still not quite quick enough as the good news is that Quasimodo takes so long making his way to the office that it gives me enough time to sneak back into the kitchen. I hold my breath as I carefully lift up one of the towels not knowing at all what to expect. My heart was racing as I looked back to the office to make sure he wouldn't catch me. You'll never believe it but under the towel was the most tiniest lamb you could possibly imagine, all warm in front of the Aga. I kid you not; it almost brought tears to my eyes. I looked back to make sure no one was coming and I lifted up another towel to find that in the next larger basket there was another two. Holy cow; I feel like I'm in a musical, with rainbows, fluffy blue skies, cute bunnies and me skipping with the lambs amongst a field of buttercups. So he does care after all but just doesn't want to admit it! I carefully lower the towel and make my way into the office to find him balancing on his tiptoes with bent knees by the filing cabinet. I actually wanted to hug him but he thinks I'm a bit of a feminist and would take great joy in having me done for sexual harassment that I'm certain. Still, he has his lambs in front of the Aga so in my eyes now; this guy can do no wrong. I kneel down by his side, completely overwhelmed and speechless, and find myself staring and smiling at him like some love sick puppy. He notes my starry eyed stare.
"What's up with thee? Looks like thaz swallowed a courgette sideways on lass."
"Nothing........just wanted to smile at you that's all." I continue to gush.
"You're not getting any funny ideas about us are ya? I know I've got a bob or too but the Mrs won't be right happy."
"Blinkin eck, can't a woman smile at a man anymore?"
"Course they can.......but not thee. Tha looks better when you're scowling at me lass," he said, ignoring my gaze and looking down at the paperwork.

I was about to protest when suddenly without any warning he loses balance off his tiptoes and falls backwards. It was a perfect backward roll, poised in its momentum with feet and knees

firmly clashed together. Then the momentum gained from the backward roll was then used to propel the forward roll, back into the original start position. It was executed smoothly and efficiently with minimal effort, precision and grace. However, due to his pride and no doubt embarrassment, he carried on as if nothing had actually happened. He stops abruptly and stares at me;
"Was thee laughing at me just then?"
"Of course not. What d'you take me for? Er, my hay fever is kicking in so I'm just going to have to nip outside a minute." I could physically feel my jaw clench as I hurriedly exited; grinning all the way to the outside porch, my stomach tightening as I attempt to contain my laughter. What the hell that was about I've no idea!

It was now dark outside despite it being only late afternoon but with very little light pollution and so I was greeted with an awesome display of twinkles from the night sky and almost a full moon as I eventually left the farm. I'm standing by two rickety gates held clumsily together by a fragile, frayed, piece of good old bailer twine. You see this type of gate construction a lot on farms; when the farmer strings two gates together to create some form of cheap barricade to help keep stock in one place. However I wasn't stood there for long when the most delightful of guests appeared by my side. You've guessed it. It's Bob! Well, it is a full moon after all so I guess it was only inevitable.
"Why it is everywhere I go, you suddenly show your kipper? You're like the eternal bad penny you are."
"I keep telling you, its fate. See those stars up there," he points; "they desperately want us together," he grinned. I roll my eyes at him. "Don't you ever wonder though, you know, what's beyond those stars?" he ponders. I think this is possibly a serious question and an attempt to be slightly intelligent. However I use the word slightly in its most loose sense.
"Well I'd imagine it's pretty much like your brain.............you know, a lot of darkness and pretty much never ending nothingness."
"Yeah, yeah, you could be right there," he nods. "I see what you're

saying."
Does nothing offend this person? I don't meet his gaze and continue to stare up to the stars. It is truly an amazing sight but I'm not indulging this joker.
"Ey, wouldn't it be romantic if a shooting star passed right now?"
"Nope."
"Would it not make you want to give us a kiss?"
"Nope."
"So would you say I'm handsome?"
"Nope."
"Have you ever thought about getting married?"
"No."
"Kids?"
"No."
"Is no, the only word you know?"
"Yep!" That's confused him!
"You do know that folk round here think you're weird."
"Well I think it's ok to be weird. We don't have to all be the same you know. Well you do, coz you're insecure."
"I'm not insecure," he says pulling up his trousers and placing both hands on his hips. Ah yes; the stance of true security. The male cowboy stance! The ultimate declaration of confidence...........not! He continues.
"Well what can I say? I'm a man who knows women," he oozes with absolute confidence.
"A man who knows women? You're joking aren't you? Even the back of a small stamp would be too large a space for you to write about the extent of your knowledge on women."
He looks at me speechless. I'm actually quite proud of my response as I'm not usually very good on the spot. I lean casually on the gate, wanting to appear casual and not at all rattled by this extremely annoying pip squeak. Oh yes, that certainly shut him up all right. And that's when it happened. It suddenly feels like the earth beneath me is moving very quickly towards my face as I land on top of the gates as they both simultaneously crash to the floor. I'm not a huge fan of expletives I have to say but they flow

quite effortlessly as I attempt to get up and retain any sense of dignity and pride I have still remaining. Bob is trying to 'help' as I grapple my way to reach an upright position.
"Is that your hand on my backside?" I ask innocently.
"Ooops! Should I remove it then?"
I glare at him. He still leaves it there.
"I'd remove it now if I was you or your highly inactive and questionable wedding tackle, gets it."
He takes a huge sigh and removes his hand, whilst grinning. I grasp the flimsy piece of bailer twine into my hands.
"How the hell is that supposed to hold up two heavy gates for goodness sake?" He continues to help me up and then suddenly I experience a sharp pain in my hip area.
"Oh! Oh! I think I've hurt my hip." I attempt to move and realise that this appears to be somewhat of a painful struggle.
"Do you want me to call for an ambulance?" asks Bob, now no longer grinning.
"No.........no, don't be bothering with all that. I'll be right in a minute. I'll try and breathe through the pain." You know what I realise in that moment? Breathing through the pain; it doesn't work. I'm now walking across the cobbled yard back to my car using my whole right side to help me drag my lower left limb.
"Bob, can you go and let Ian know that I've had to go home?"
"Don't you think you should be going to t'hospital?"
"No! No! No need for that. I'm not using valuable NHS resources for a minor injury like this," I snap.

I'm now clambering into my car by the way and I have to physically lift my leg in as my hip appears unable to carry the weight of it.
"You can't be driving like that," says Bob.
"Stop your fussing will you. It's fine. If it ain't broke; don't fix it. That's my motto!"
Ian suddenly slopes up to the car.
"She's hurt her hip. Fell down on them there gates. She won't go to t'hospital to get it checked," shouts Bob over the car bonnet to

Ian.

Ian stares at me, straight faced and says absolutely nothing. I'm struggling to meet his gaze. There has always been a very fine line between his smile and a grimace but in the corner of my eye I'm definitely picking up the vibes of a grin. He turns briskly away. I don't know why he's moving so quickly as he slopes off into the dark shadows, towards the silo tower. It's not like its bell ringing night or anything. I wind down the car window a bit further and lean out shouting;

"Ey, I hope you're not laughing at me?" I shout. He doesn't even turn round which I find rude and infuriating. "Ey, can you hear me?" I shout again, "I said can you hear me? Are you listening to me? Are you........Oh forget it! I may as well be talking to my bloody self!"

Hope you enjoyed my book. If you did, please could you click the star rating on Amazon or if you have time, write a short review. This helps more people read the book which means the book then becomes more popular. This hopefully will put a smile on more people's faces. Many thanks for your support and do look out for The Yorkshire Misfit Book 3. Champion!

Printed in Poland
by Amazon Fulfillment
Poland Sp. z o.o., Wrocław

51089704R00040